WILLIAM SHAKESPEARE'S

Twelfth Night

retold by Bruce Coville
illustrated by Tim Raglin

Dial Books · New York

For Naomi Miller
—B.C.

A fitting tribute to E. L. Wempe, not?
—T.R.

Published by Dial Books
A division of Penguin Putnam Inc.
345 Hudson Street
New York, New York 10014
Designed by Lily Malcom
Text set in MBell
Manufactured in China on acid-free paper
1 3 5 7 9 10 8 6 4 2
Library of Congress Cataloging-in-Publication Data
Coville, Bruce.
William Shakespeare's Twelfth night / retold by Bruce Coville ;
illustrated by Tim Raglin.
p.   cm.
ISBN 0-8037-2318-0
1. Shakespeare, William, 1564–1616—Adaptations—Juvenile
literature. 2. Survival after airplane accidents, shipwrecks,
etc.—Juvenile fiction. 3. Brothers and sisters—Juvenile fiction.
4. Illyria—Juvenile fiction. 5. Twins—Juvenile fiction. [1. Shakespeare,
William, 1564–1616—Adaptations.]   I. Raglin, Tim, ill.
II. Shakespeare, William, 1564–1616. Twelfth night. III. Title.
PR2878.T8 C67 2003
822'.3'3—dc21
2001028252

The artwork for this book was created
in pen and inks on illustration board.

AUTHOR'S NOTE

Though four centuries old, *Twelfth Night* has never lost its capacity to delight. While there is no magic as such in the play, it still has an almost fairy tale quality, as if we have entered an enchanted world.

Among high school groups, *Twelfth Night* remains one of the most read and performed of Shakespeare's plays—and with good reason. One of the "joyous comedies," it is packed with concerns that go straight to the heart of young readers. Viola, finding herself out of place and alone in the world, tries on a new identity. She becomes tangled in the knot of her deception, yearning for someone who is nearby but to whom she dares not speak her love. It is the struggle of adolescence in microcosm!

The play is almost perfectly balanced, in that the comic subplot receives as much time as the romantic leads. (Indeed, on stage, Sir Toby and company can easily steal the show.) So completely are these plots woven together that it is hard to pluck one thread without unraveling the whole fabric. While it is sometimes possible, even necessary, to delete subplots for these adaptations, in this case every element of the story is intact.

It is unfortunate that the sense of "high culture" we have wrapped around Shakespeare's work often obscures the raucous and delightful reality of a play such as this, and frightens readers and playgoers—both young and old—from sampling its pleasures. In the case of *Twelfth Night* the title alone is a clue to its celebratory nature, for while it has nothing to do with the plot or the characters, it has all to do with both festivity and the end of festival, the restoration of order, which occurs when the wild misunderstandings of the play are brought to a finish and harmony returns. (The actual holiday of Twelfth Night falls on January 6, and once marked the end of the Christmas/New Year season.)

As with the other volumes in this line, our hope with this book is to provide a hint of the happy experience awaiting young audiences when they enter the world of the Bard. In short, this is not meant as a replacement for the original, but as an appetizer for the greater feast still to come.

In ancient Illyria lived a duke named Orsino who pined for the love of a noblewoman named Olivia.

Alas, Olivia loved him not.

Moping in his courtroom, Orsino cried to his musicians, "If music be the food of love, play on! Give me more than I can hold. Perhaps then this appetite will sicken and die."

So he sat, wrapped in music and sorrow, waiting for the messenger he had sent to carry his words of love to Olivia. But when the man returned, he shook his head sadly. "She would not even let me in. Her handmaid says the lady mourns her brother's recent death, and will do so for seven years."

The duke groaned, but still hoped to turn Olivia's heart. "If she pays such a debt of love to but a brother, how much more might she love a man such as me?"

Not far away another young woman also mourned a lost brother. This was Viola, who had washed up on Illyria's coast after a shipwreck. Alas, her twin, Sebastian, was nowhere to be seen.

"Take heart," said the captain of the sunken vessel, who had also made it to shore. "Your brother may yet live. After our ship did split, I saw him bind himself to a strong mast."

"May that be so!" cried Viola. She glanced around fearfully. "Know you this country?"

"I was born not three hours' travel from this beach. The land is governed by a noble duke, Orsino by name. When I set sail, it was rumored he sought the love of Lady Olivia. But she is lost in mourning and will not answer him."

Viola sighed. "Would that I served that lady, and might weep with her until my own situation comes clear. It is not good for a woman to be alone in a strange land."

"Olivia's home would be a safe place for you," agreed the captain. "But the lady gives audience to no one."

"Then mayhap it is the duke I should serve."

"He has no women in his court!" said the startled captain.

"Then I will come to him disguised as a man," replied Viola, seized by her idea. "I can sing to him in many sorts of music that will make me worthy of his service."

With the captain's help Viola cut her long hair and put on men's attire. Then they traveled to the court of Duke Orsino, where the captain introduced her as "Cesario."

As time passed, Orsino found something strangely appealing about this Cesario, who listened so much more sympathetically than his other men. Soon he decided the newcomer should be the one to carry his latest message of love to Olivia. Taking the youth by the hand, the duke said urgently, "I have unclasped the secret book of my soul to you. Carry those words to her I love. Stand rooted at her door until you are granted audience. She will attend you better for thy youth."

"I think not so, my lord," said Viola modestly.

"Dear lad, believe it. Your youth gives you a beauty that is almost . . . womanly. It will soften her."

"I'll do my best," promised Viola. But her heart was heavy, for she herself was falling in love with the duke!

As for the Lady Olivia, her mourning was made more difficult by her drunken uncle, Sir Toby Belch, who had brought to the household a tall and tremulous suitor named Sir Andrew Aguecheek. Like Orsino, Sir Andrew hoped to win the hand of Olivia—a task made more difficult in *his* case by the fact that he was a coward and a fool. But he had a great deal of money to spend, so Sir Toby happily encouraged the hopeless suit.

Olivia's maid, Maria, as clever as Sir Andrew was dull, tolerated their presence for another reason: She had a secret liking for Sir Toby.

It was Maria who brought word that a handsome youth stood at the gates, wishing to speak to Olivia.

"What is he who is at the gate?" Olivia asked Sir Toby, who had staggered in behind Maria.

"A (hic) gentleman," said Sir Toby. He covered his mouth. "A plague on these pickled herrings!" he cried, trying to pretend he had not been drinking.

Before he could say more, Olivia's steward, Malvolio, came bustling in. He was a sour man, with no taste for Sir Toby's foolery.

"Malvolio, what can *you* tell me of this caller?" asked Olivia, who was beginning to grow exasperated.

"Not yet old enough for a man, nor young enough for a boy," said Malvolio, sniffing a bit. "One would think his mother's milk were scarce out of him. Yet he stands like a post at the gate, and claims he will not be moved until you see him."

Intrigued, Olivia said, "Let him approach. Maria, bring my veil that I might hide my face."

When Viola entered, she began eagerly, "Most radiant, exquisite, and unmatchable beauty—" She stopped and turned to Maria. "Pray, tell me if this be the lady of the house. I would hate to cast away my speech."

"I am that lady," said Olivia. "You may pass over the empty praise."

Viola shook her head. "Alas, I took great pains to study it, and 'tis poetical. But it is secret, and concerns your ear alone."

Something in the youth's manner appealed to Olivia, so she sent Maria away. Then, at Viola's request, she removed her veil. Viola's heart sank when she saw Olivia's beauty. Yet she did not turn from her mission. Speaking with honesty and passion about the duke's love, she chastised Olivia for being hard-hearted. "If I did love you in my master's flame— with such suffering, such passion—then in your denial I would find no sense."

"What would you do?" asked Olivia.

"Make me a willow cabin at your gate. Write aching songs of rejected love and sing them loud. Cry your name to the echoing hills, until the babbling gossip of the air replied 'Olivia, Olivia, Olivia!'"

With these words and more, Viola moved Olivia's heart, but not in the way she intended. No sooner had the lady dismissed the handsome lad than she longed to see him again. Pulling a ring from her finger, she called Malvolio and said, "That peevish messenger left this token. Tell him I won't take it, and if he'll come this way tomorrow, I'll tell him why." With this ruse, she hoped to bring the youth back.

Eager to please his lady, Malvolio hurried after "Cesario." When the youth would not accept the ring, Malvolio flung it to the ground. "If it be worth stooping for, there it lies!" he snapped. Then he stalked away, huffing indignantly.

Viola knelt to retrieve the ring, and with a sudden chill realized what it meant. Clutching it to her breast, she murmured, "Disguise, I see thou art a wickedness. Look what now has come to pass. I love my master, who knows not I am a woman. He in turn loves Olivia. And she, thinking me a man, has come to dote on me instead of him! O Time, thou must untangle this, not I; it is too hard a knot for me to untie."

Late that night Sir Toby and Sir Andrew were carousing in the kitchen of Olivia's house with Olivia's fool, Feste.

"A song!" demanded the drunken knights. "A song!"

Though Feste's song was sweet and mellow, the knights were soon bellowing along. Maria rushed in to quiet them, but had no success, and soon was laughing with them.

Their merriment was cut short when Malvolio came stalking into the kitchen in his nightgown. "Do you make an alehouse of my lady's house?" he cried indignantly.

Sir Toby tipsily drew himself to his full height. "Dost thou (hic) think because thou art (hic) virtuous, there shall be no more cakes and ale?"

"My lady shall know of this!" warned Malvolio.

The steward stormed out of the room, leaving Toby and Andrew fuming over his high-handed ways. But Maria said slyly, "I know a way to put this Malvolio in his place."

"What wilt thou do?" asked Toby eagerly.

Leaning close, she whispered, "I can write so like my lady that sometimes we ourselves cannot tell our hands apart. I shall write a letter as if from her, in which our Malvolio will find himself much praised. When I drop it in his path, what an ass might he not make of himself?"

In Orsino's court, melancholy music again filled the air.

"What think you of this tune, Cesario?" the duke asked Viola.

"It gives a very echo to the seat where love is throned," she replied.

Orsino smiled sadly. "Upon my life I would say that you loved someone yourself. Come, boy, what is she like?"

Viola, indeed aching with love, replied, "One who looks much like you."

"She is not worth thee, then! What of her years?"

"About your years, my lord."

"Too old, by heaven!"

No, thought Viola, just right. But she dared not speak what was in her heart, which grew even heavier when Orsino asked her to carry yet another message of love to Olivia.

"But if she cannot love you, sir?"

The duke's face hardened. "I cannot be so answered."

Viola lowered her eyes. "Say some lady has for you as great a pang of heart as you have for Olivia. You cannot love her. You tell her so. Must she not be so answered?"

"There is no woman could hold the beating of so strong a passion as love doth give my heart!"

"Yet I know too well what love women may feel," said Viola gently. "My father had a daughter loved a man—as it might be, perhaps, were I a woman, I should love your lordship."

"And what's her history?"

"She never told her love, but let concealment, like a worm in the bud, feed on her damask cheek. She sat like Patience on a monument, smiling at grief. Was not this love indeed? We men may say more, swear more; but still we prove much in our vows, but little in our love."

"But died thy sister of her love, boy?"

"I am all the daughters of my father's house, and all the brothers too. And yet, I know not."

At Olivia's, Maria dropped her letter on a path in the garden where she knew Malvolio was sure to find it. Sir Toby and Sir Andrew, giggling like schoolboys, hid in the shrubbery to see what would happen when he read it.

Soon their enemy came wandering down the path. Spying the letter, he bent to pick it up.

"By my life," he murmured, "this is my lady's handwriting! And it is addressed to . . . to the Unknown Beloved!"

Trembling with excitement, Malvolio opened the letter, which Maria had cunningly written to convince him he was indeed loved by Olivia. Toby and Andrew nearly burst with glee as the steward read aloud, "In my stars I am above thee, but be not afraid of greatness. Some are born great, some achieve greatness, and some have greatness thrust upon 'em."

Malvolio read on. The letter encouraged him to dress in yellow stockings with crisscrossing garters, to create trouble with Sir Toby, and to come smiling before Olivia—all as ways to show his love. Completely taken in, the steward fairly skipped down the path as he hurried to follow the letter's commands. Had he waited but a moment longer, he would have seen Sir Toby and Sir Andrew stagger out of the bushes, laughing so hard they had to hold each other up.

The mischievous knights composed themselves as they saw Duke Orsino's young messenger approaching. But when Olivia hurried out to greet "Cesario" with warm smiles, Sir Andrew grew jealous—a jealousy that flamed into anger when Olivia said, "Let the garden door be shut and leave me with my messenger."

As soon as the two knights were gone, Olivia unburdened her heart. "O Cesario!" she cried, embracing the youth. "By the roses of spring, by maidhood, honor, truth, and everything, I love thee so that neither wit nor reason can hide it."

Alarmed, Viola slid from Olivia's arms. "I have one heart, one bosom, and one truth, and that no woman has, nor never none shall mistress be of it, save I alone." Then she fled, leaving Olivia burning with love.

In another part of Illyria stood a young man who much resembled Viola, and with good reason: He was her lost twin, Sebastian, who had stayed afloat on his mast until a passing vessel pulled him from the water.

The captain of that ship, Antonio by name, had grown so fond of Sebastian he had decided to travel with the youth for a time.

"Come, friend," urged Sebastian now, "let's explore this city."

Antonio shook his head. "This is Duke Orsino's country. Once in a sea fight I did much damage against his ships. Were I found here, it would go hard with me. I'll wait at our lodging place. Take my purse; I'll have little need of it, and you may have cause to open it as you travel."

"I shall meet you at the inn," promised Sebastian.

Olivia had sent some of her servants to fetch Cesario back. As she sat waiting with Maria, secretly fretting about how best to woo the lad, Malvolio came strutting before her dressed in yellow stockings with crossed garters. Even stranger, he was . . . smiling.

"What is the matter with thee?" cried Olivia.

"Ah," said Malvolio. "'Be not afraid of greatness.' That was well writ. 'Some are born great. Some achieve greatness. And some have greatness thrust upon them.'" Then he grinned even more broadly.

"Heaven restore thy wits!" said Olivia in alarm.

"I know who likes yellow stockings," said Malvolio, winking at her as he extended his leg. "I know who wished to see me cross-gartered!"

At that moment a servant announced that Cesario had returned.

"Maria!" cried Olivia. "Fetch Sir Toby and tell him to look after Malvolio." Then she hurried off to see Cesario.

"She sends for her kinsman so that I can fulfill her command to be cross with him!" Malvolio told himself happily. And when Maria returned with Sir Toby, the steward did just that. "Be gone. I discard you!" he said, and stalked away.

"Rarely has fish swallowed bait so deeply," gloated Sir Toby. "My niece already fears he is mad, which is all the excuse we need now to bind him in a dark room."

Before they could leave, Sir Andrew came loping in. "I've written a challenge to Cesario!" he announced, thrusting a paper at Sir Toby.

Toby scanned the note, then said solemnly, "I myself will take this to the youth. Await him at the corner of the meadow."

When Andrew was gone, Sir Toby tore up the note. "It stinks of cowardice," he whispered to Maria. "But the report of Andrew's ferocity I shall pour into Cesario's ear will make *his* fear equal to Andrew's. By the time they meet, both will be so afraid, they may kill each other with a look!" Maria, who loved mischief as much as Toby did, laughed merrily at the idea.

Viola, already shaken by Olivia's avowal of love, was doubly distressed when Sir Toby hurried up to her and boomed, "You have offended the mighty Sir Andrew! He waits for you, sword ready to regain lost honor."

"I have done him no harm!" cried Viola.

"He says otherwise. And I must warn you, he is a devil in private brawl who has already divided three men body from soul."

"I will return to the house," said Viola.

"To do so would be to forsake all pride. But, out of pity, I will approach the knight on your behalf."

What Toby *actually* told Sir Andrew, of course, was that "Cesario" was eager to fight. By the time he brought the terrified combatants together, Andrew was quaking with fear and Viola was almost ready to admit she was a girl in disguise.

Never did two swords clash with less enthusiasm. Indeed, they barely touched, as each fighter was terrified of angering the other. Struggling not to laugh, Toby urged the trembling fighters on. But suddenly a man rushed between them.

It was Antonio, who had grown worried about Sebastian and come looking for him. Seeing Viola disguised as a man, the captain had taken her for her twin.

"Put up your sword!" he roared at Sir Andrew. "If this young gentleman have done offense, I take the fault on me."

The hubbub attracted some of Orsino's officers, who came to stop the fight. One recognized Antonio; clapping a hand upon his shoulder, he declared, "I arrest you as an enemy of the duke!"

To Viola's astonishment Antonio turned to her and said, "Alas, I must now ask back the money I recently gave you."

"What money?" she asked, completely baffled.

"Will you deny me?" cried Antonio. "After I snatched you out of the jaws of death?"

Before Viola could ask what Antonio meant, the guards dragged him away. Had she been on the other side of the manor, she might have understood better, for when Olivia sent Feste to fetch "Cesario" back, the clown had spotted Sebastian on the street. Seeing the twin and assuming he had found his man, Feste had convinced Sebastian to come to the house.

When Sir Andrew saw Sebastian, he fell into the same error. Made bold by Viola's earlier timidity, he cried, "So, we meet again!" and launched a new attack. But unlike Viola, Sebastian was a trained fighter.

"Why, there's for thee!" he answered, striking back angrily. "Take that! And that!"

Sir Andrew tumbled to the ground. Sir Toby drew his own sword, but before he could strike, Olivia came upon the scene. Seeing her uncle about to attack the youth she loved (or so she thought), she cried, "Ungracious wretch! Leave my sight!"

Toby slunk away, taking Sir Andrew with him. "Be not offended, dear Cesario," pleaded Olivia, clutching Sebastian by the arm.

Sebastian had no idea why this beautiful lady was calling him Cesario. But he hardly wished to offend her. "If I am dreaming, let me sleep on," he murmured as he followed her to her garden.

As the day drew on, Maria's jest with Malvolio took a cruel turn. The pranksters, claiming the steward was mad, had locked him in a dark room. Now Sir Toby sent Feste, disguised as a parson, to visit him, and hid nearby to listen.

When Malvolio heard Feste's footsteps approaching, he called, "Who is there?"

Disguising his voice with a quaver, Feste replied, "It is Sir Topas the curate—come to visit Malvolio the lunatic."

"Sir Topas!" cried Malvolio desperately. "Go to my lady!"

"Ack!" cried Feste, still pretending to be a parson. "He is possessed by a demon! He can speak of nothing but ladies."

"Sir Topas, good Sir Topas! Do not think I am mad. They have laid me here in hideous darkness."

Though Malvolio was indeed locked in total darkness, Feste said, "Fie, you have huge windows!"

"I say this house is dark as ignorance," wailed Malvolio.

Sir Toby was enjoying the prank immensely. But he knew it would make his niece more cross with him than she was already, so after a while he whispered to Feste, "Now speak to him in your own voice."

Feste began to sing. Though Malvolio had never liked the clown, he called plaintively, "Dear friend fool!"

"Alas, sir," replied Feste, pretending to be surprised to find the steward here, "how fell you out of your wits?"

"I am as well in my wits, fool, as thou art."

"You are mad indeed if you be no better in your wits than a fool," said Feste gleefully. But at last he relented and at Malvolio's pleading brought paper, ink, and a lamp, so the poor man could write to Olivia.

While Malvolio struggled to convince his tormentors he was sane, Sebastian was wondering if *he* had gone mad. Why would a beautiful lady pluck him from a brawl and offer to make him her husband? Yet the air, the sun, the very pearl the lady had just given him felt real enough.

"How I wish Antonio were here," he said. "His counsel now might do me golden service." But he was too lost in enchantment to spend much thought on worry.

And when Olivia returned to the garden with a priest at her side and said, "If you mean well, come with me and this holy man, and pledge me your love, that my jealous and doubtful soul may live at peace," Sebastian went gladly to be married.

Duke Orsino, weary of awaiting an answer from Olivia, decided to visit her himself. He brought along his court, including "Cesario." But as they approached Olivia's house, the guards who had captured Antonio arrived with their prisoner.

"Look, my lord!" cried Viola. "It is the man I told you of—the one that did rescue me."

"I know that face as well," said Orsino darkly. "He is an old enemy. Well, thou saltwater thief—what foolish boldness brings you here?"

"A witchcraft, cast by that ungrateful boy who stands beside you," Antonio replied, pointing to Viola. "I pulled him from the sea's mouth, and for three months we have kept close company. For his sake came I into the danger of this town."

"Madness!" snapped Orsino. "For three months this youth has tended upon me. Take him away. My lady approaches."

But Olivia walked past Orsino to take Cesario by the arm.

"Still so cruel?" asked the duke.

"Still so constant," replied Olivia.

Orsino, enraged, took Cesario's other arm. "Come, boy," he snarled. "We'll stay no more here."

"Stay, my husband Cesario!" cried Olivia.

"Husband?" roared the astonished duke.

"Yes, husband," said Olivia firmly.

"Not I!" protested Viola in horror.

"That is your fear speaking," chided Olivia. Turning to one of her servants, she said, "Call forth the holy father!"

When the priest came and swore he had indeed joined Olivia and Cesario in marriage, it was all the duke could do to keep from strangling his messenger. "To plot and lie so smoothly while still so young," he raged. "What monster will you be when you are older?"

"My lord, I do protest!" cried Viola.

At that moment Sir Andrew came stumbling among them. Feste followed closely, holding up a drunk and staggering Sir Toby. "This youth Cesario has broke my head," wailed Sir Andrew. "Yes, and gave Toby a bloody coxcomb too."

"*My* Cesario?" asked Orsino, more astonished than ever.

"I never hurt you, Sir Andrew!" cried Viola. "You drew your sword on me without cause, but no blows fell between us."

Toby burped and fell over.

Sir Andrew bent to help him, but Toby—who had finally grown tired of the foolish knight—pushed him away.

"Get him to bed, and let his hurt be looked to," ordered the baffled Olivia.

As the servants dragged Sir Toby off, Sebastian came strolling in.
"Madam, I am sorry I hurt your kinsman, but—" He broke off when he
saw the look of wonder on Olivia's face. Then he noticed Antonio. "My
dear friend!" he cried joyfully.

"An apple cleft in two is not more twin than these two creatures," whispered Antonio in wonder. "Which is Sebastian?"

Then Viola stepped forward, and Sebastian saw the cause of all the amazement and confusion.

Unable to believe such joy was possible, he said cautiously, "I never had a brother. I did have a sister, but her the blind waves and surges have devoured. Of what country are you, what name, what parentage?"

"Of Messaline," replied Viola with equal caution. "Sebastian was my father. So too was named my brother, who went to a watery tomb."

"Were you a woman, I should my tears let fall on your cheek," whispered Sebastian. "And say, 'Thrice welcome, drowned Viola!'"

Tears trembling in her own eyes, Viola answered, "If nothing stands between our happiness but these men's clothes, then know I only donned them so I might serve this noble duke."

Orsino came to Viola's side and said tenderly, "Thou has said a thousand times thou should never love woman the way you love me."

"And all those swearings I will swear again!" Viola exclaimed.

"Give me thy hand," said Orsino. "And let me see thee in thy woman's weeds."

"The captain who has my maid's garments is held in jail at some charge laid by Malvolio," said Viola sadly.

"Malvolio!" cried Olivia. "In my own near madness, I had forgotten him. Alas, I fear he may not be in his right mind."

Feste chose this moment to give Malvolio's letter to Olivia. "Fetch him here," she ordered as soon as she read it.

"Madam, you have done me wrong!" cried Malvolio when he was brought among them.

"How mean you?" asked Olivia.

"Study this," he said, handing her Maria's note. "Did you not write this, and bid me come smiling and cross-gartered before you, to put on yellow stockings, and to frown upon Sir Toby? And when I did all as you asked, was I not locked away in a dark house? Tell me why!"

Olivia studied the note, then said gently, "This is not my writing, Malvolio. Much like it, I confess. But without doubt, it is Maria's hand."

Then Feste, who never minded landing in a bit of trouble for the sake of a jest, explained the entire prank. ". . . And in return for Maria writing the letter," he concluded, "Sir Toby has gone and married her!"

"Alas, poor fool," said Olivia, extending her hand to Malvolio, "how have they baffled thee!"

"Some are born great, some achieve greatness, and some have greatness thrust upon 'em," cried Feste merrily, putting on the voice of Sir Topas.

Malvolio's eyes widened in outrage. "I'll be revenged on the whole pack of you!" he screamed. Then he stormed away.

"He hath been most notoriously abused," said Olivia.

Orsino turned to his men. "Pursue him and entreat him to a peace. Learn what we need do to free Viola's captain."

Then he offered Viola his arm, and he and Olivia led the reunited brother and sister into the great house, where there began a celebration that echoed in joy down all the days of their lives.